Aisha Bushby was born in the Middle East and now lives in the UK. When she's not reading or writing stories, she likes playing cosy video games, watching animated films, and working on her miniature house.

Kübra Teber lives in Ayvalık, Turkey. She likes reading, travelling, walking, finding antiques in flea markets and nature. She loves picnics most of all.

T0371022

First published in the UK in 2023 by Usborne Publishing Limited, Usborne House,

83-85 Saffron Hill, London EC1N 8RT, England. usborne.com

Usborne Verlag, Usborne Publishing Ltd., Prüfeninger Str. 20,
93049 Regensburg, Deutschland, VK Nr. 17560

Text copyright © Aisha Bushby, 2023

The right of Aisha Bushby to be identified as the author of this work has been asserted by her
in accordance with the Copyright, Designs and Patents Act, 1988.

Illustrations by Kübra Teber © Usborne Publishing Limited, 2023.

The name Usborne and the Balloon logo are trade marks of Usborne Publishing Limited.

All rights reserved. No part of this publication may be reproduced or used in any manner for
the purpose of training artificial intelligence technologies or systems (including for text or
data mining), stored in retrieval systems or transmitted in any form or by any means without
prior permission of the publisher.

This is a work of fiction. The characters, incidents, and dialogues are products of the author's
imagination and are not to be construed as real. Any resemblance to actual events or persons,
living or dead, is entirely coincidental.

A CIP catalogue record for this book is available from the British Library.

JFM MJJASOND/25 7639/2 ISBN 9781801314121

Printed and bound using 100% renewable energy at CPI Group (UK) Ltd, Croydon, CR0 4YY.

TINY the Secret Adventurer

Aisha Bushby

illustrated by **Kübra Teber**

USBORNE

Contents

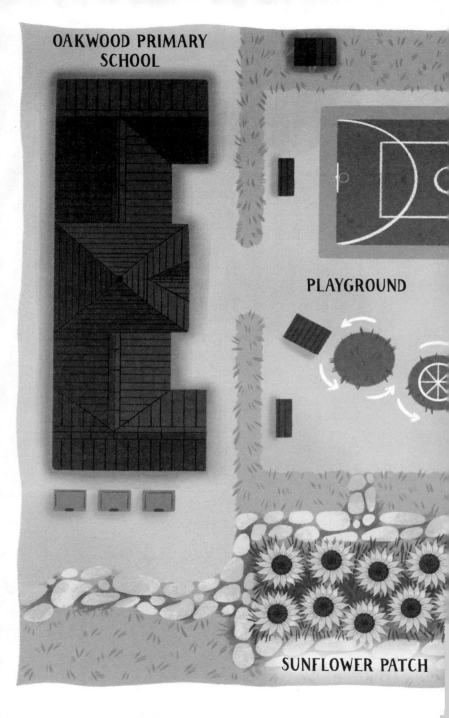

FROG'S HOLLOW

GARDEN SHED

WILDFLOWER MEADOW

VEGETABLE PATCH

WOODS

BLUEBERRY BUSH

GRASSLAND

How it Began

It all started with a seed, lovingly planted and watered at Oakwood Primary School.

At one end of the school garden was the sunflower patch, and at the other was Frog's Hollow, where a pond was surrounded by tall grass. In between there were grasslands, a blueberry bush, woods, a wildflower meadow and a vegetable patch. Each part of the garden was like a different colour of the rainbow.

After several weeks the sunflower seeds, watched closely by the children every day at break times, grew into shoots. These sprouted into leaves and then the colourful heads of sunflowers. Their petals were clasped shut.

The sunflowers grew
and grew and grew until
the flowers reached
the height of the
children's knees.
They grew past their
shoulders, eventually
stretching as tall as
the children. It was
when the sunflowers
were taller than even
the tallest child, that
the flowers began to
bloom. Their petals were
as bright as the sun.

Only one flower – the smallest of the bunch – bloomed with something extra special…

A little creature, born early one morning, before school began. She was just getting used to her surroundings when the children arrived.

"That one's tiny!" said a child, pointing at the special sunflower with the brightest petals. It was this sunflower that housed the little creature never seen before in the school garden. The creature, who resembled a human child in every way apart from her size, decided that this would become her name: Tiny.

Tiny stood as tall as your forefinger, with wavy brown hair that fell down to her chin, and brown skin and eyes too.

And though she was only little, the adventures she went on in the school garden were rather big and scary and exciting.

CHAPTER 1

Tiny

Tiny liked the sound a book made as the page turned. It swished, like a bird's wings flapping through the air. Quietly, so the human girl who was reading it didn't hear her, Tiny scuttled forward. She wanted to peer at the book up close. It had lots of pictures inside it, sketched in black and white.

Tiny couldn't
read along
with the
human girl
because
the words
were
strange
symbols
that she didn't
recognize. And they
wriggled around like worms. But Tiny
could hear the girl whisper them aloud,
and she drank them in like they were
dewdrops on a cold morning.

Words, Tiny decided, were her favourite things – beside the taste of delicious blueberries and the sight of bright butterfly wings – and she tried her best to remember the ones that sounded fun in her mouth.

"Nour," an older human said as they approached the girl. "What are you reading today?"

Nour, thought Tiny. *That's a nice-sounding name.* But then she realized the older human would see her unless she hid very quickly. And so she scrambled away from the edge of the playground and into the sunflower patch, hiding among the stalks and leaves.

Just before she started reading her book, Nour had tended to Tiny's sunflower the way she did every morning before the bell rang. Sometimes she stopped ants from climbing up the sunflower stalks and eating its petals. And other times, on a hot day like today, she watered the sunflower to keep it nourished.

Nour shared Tiny's brown skin,
but she had long brown hair twisted
together in two plaits. Where Tiny's
clothes were made from bright sweet
wrappers and other things Tiny had
found in the garden, Nour wore a white
T-shirt and grey shorts, with white
stripy socks and white shoes.

Other children were there, all
wearing the same white and grey
clothes. Dozens of them ran around the
playground of Oakwood Primary, dust
flying up from their shoes. Tiny knew
never *ever* to cross the playground,
or else she might be squashed. These

humans were different to Nour, making lots of noise, screaming and laughing as they ran.

Tiny spent most of her days alone in the sunflower patch, occasionally spying a mouse. They seemed sweet, with their grey fur and beady eyes. And best of all they were just her size!

Tiny wanted to play with the mice the way the children played together. She was lonely by herself and she wondered what it would be like to have a friend. Or at least someone to talk to.

Little did she know that her small world was going to grow bigger than she could have imagined, and her life would soon be filled with lots of chatter and excitement... Though perhaps not in the way she had hoped.

CHAPTER 2

The Mice

When the school bell rang the sound rumbled along the ground, shaking beneath Tiny's feet. Every time it happened, it made her skin prickle and her bones rattle. She covered her ears and scrunched her eyes shut to block it out.

When she opened them again, the children were lined up like ants in neat rows. Tiny could see Nour among them with her head down and her book cradled to her chest.

One by one, the children stepped inside the great building. Tiny knew they would be back when the next bell rang and, once again, they would scatter around the playground and scream and laugh in chorus.

For now, Tiny enjoyed the peace and quiet: the wind as it rustled through the leaves, and the sing-song chirp of birds. She peered up at the sunflowers, enjoying the way the petals fluttered in the gentle breeze. Usually, at this point, she would

climb back up
her sunflower
and bathe
in the sun,
but it was
too hot
to do that
today, so she
decided to try
something different.

With the humans all inside, the school

garden came to life as the animals came

out to explore. Birds landed on the

playground to peck at crumbs on the

tarmac. Splashes could be heard all the

way across the school garden from Frog's Hollow. And from somewhere nearby came tittering noises.

The mice! thought Tiny, excitedly. *Maybe today is the day I'll introduce myself to them.*

She crept along the soil, suddenly feeling a little shy as she approached and watched them play a funny little game. Two mice were holding either end of a long blade of grass. They twirled it in the air while a third mouse jumped up and over it.

Tiny had seen the humans play a similar game in the playground, and she thought it looked fun.

"Can I join in?" Tiny asked bravely,
stepping forward from her hiding place.

The mice all stopped what they were
doing, dropped the blade of grass and
stared at her curiously.

"Who are you?" said the first mouse, its
nose twitching as it sniffed at her.

"What are you wearing?" asked the second, approaching Tiny slowly on its pitter-patter feet. The other mice followed behind.

"*What* are you?" said the third mouse, eyeing up Tiny's sweet-wrapper clothes. "Why haven't you got any fur?"

The first mouse pulled at Tiny's hair. "This is sort of like fur," it said. "But not quite."

The mice had surrounded Tiny now, and she was no longer excited. She had a funny feeling in her tummy that twisted and turned with fear.

"Stop it!" Tiny said, pulling her hair away from the first mouse while the third mouse poked at her arm. The second mouse spoke again.

"You can't play with us," it said, standing as tall as it could.

"Yeah!" said the first mouse. "Leave us alone!"

"Go away," said the third mouse,

shoving Tiny so she fell to the floor,

landing on her bum.

Tiny was so

shocked that

she didn't say

anything or

move. Then

tears sprang

to her eyes and the

funny feeling in her tummy burst like an

overripe blueberry.

The mice stood there, watching her,

until Tiny pulled herself up and ran quickly

back to her sunflower.

CHAPTER 3
I'm Not Silly

Tiny made it up
the first three
leaves of the
sunflower stalk,
placing
a foot on either
side to climb it.
Her whole body

31

was shaking as she recovered from how mean the mice had been. But then leaves below started to rustle.

Tiny peered down to see all three mice had surrounded her sunflower. They were going to follow her up!

She managed to climb up a few more leaves. Tiny glanced back to see the mice were much slower than she was, and felt a little proud, even though she was still upset. This was her sunflower and she knew it better than they did.

The next bit she needed to climb was tricky, because the leaf she wanted was on the other side of the sunflower stem and her arms couldn't reach for it from where she was standing.

She would have to leap for it.

Tiny paused, crouched down, and counted to three – *One, two, three!* Then, she jumped as high as she could, just managing to grab the next leaf and pull herself up.

Tiny peered down to
see, rustling among
the lower leaves,
the three little
mice staring up
at her. They
watched
with beady eyes, their
whiskers twitching. They were all
giggling at her in a way that made her want
to cry again.

"What's so funny?" asked Tiny,
confused.

"You," said the first mouse.

"Yes, you!" added the second. "You

climb in such
a funny way,
leaping all
over the place."

"Silly human,"
said the third
mouse.

Tiny frowned.
"I'm not a human," she answered, before
adding, "and I'm not silly."

"Oh yes you are!" said the second mouse,
and Tiny wasn't sure whether they were
saying she was a human or silly. Either way
she felt a strange prickling in her chest that
now replaced the funny feeling in her belly.

It was like the sun was burning inside her. Her face grew hot and she had the urge to yell at the mice. So she did.

"Stop saying that and leave me alone!" Tiny felt like wind was gushing around inside her chest, making her voice louder and louder. "And get away from my sunflower. It's *mine* and I haven't invited you over."

"You're going to fall," said the first mouse, ignoring her. "*SPLAT* like a blueberry."

For some reason this made the mice giggle even more, until their mothers arrived and ushered them away. The grown-up mice glared up at Tiny as if *she* was the one who had been mean.

Though the mice had gone, the strange prickly feeling lingered in Tiny's chest. She used it to push herself up and up and up, until she was standing atop her sunflower safe from the dangers of the world below.

CHAPTER 4

The Animals

The sunflowers were even more beautiful
when you looked at them from here, tilting
forward to kiss the sun. Tiny's own
sunflower stood steady beneath her feet,
and there was a lovely spot where she
could settle safely among its bright yellow
petals. Tiny watched as lots of little
bumblebees bounced between the

sunflowers, one of them visiting hers.

"Hello!" said Tiny, not minding when it didn't reply.

The bumblebee walked
round the brown bud,
collecting bits of pollen in its
hair, before flying off.

"Goodbye!" said Tiny,
grateful for all that the
bumblebee did to keep the
school garden alive.

Tiny noticed a change in the
school garden all of a sudden.
She peered around. The
splashing in the pond that Tiny

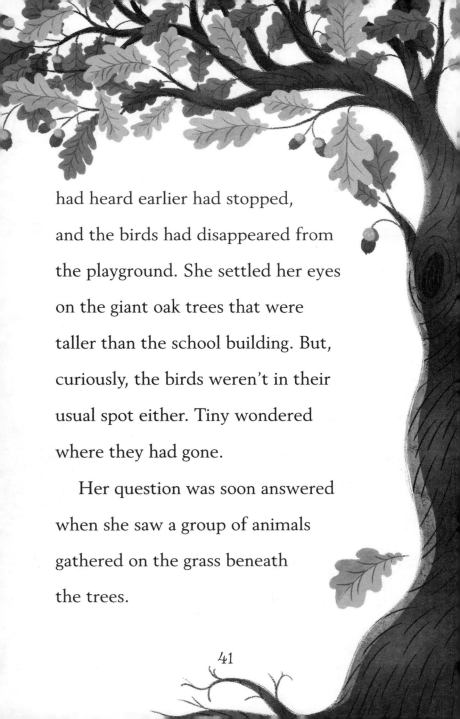

had heard earlier had stopped, and the birds had disappeared from the playground. She settled her eyes on the giant oak trees that were taller than the school building. But, curiously, the birds weren't in their usual spot either. Tiny wondered where they had gone.

Her question was soon answered when she saw a group of animals gathered on the grass beneath the trees.

First, there were the birds, lined up on a low branch. Next, there were the mice, clustered just beyond the sunflowers. And there were two other animals standing alone. A grey squirrel and a frog. None of the animals looked comfortable in each

other's presence, as they settled far apart from one another. Tiny could hear them arguing through the breeze that carried their voices. But she was too far away to make out what they were saying.

"I wonder what they're talking about," Tiny muttered, feeling a little left out. She lived in these parts too. Why hadn't she been invited to meet them?

Tiny decided to find out what they were saying, so she leaped and hopped from sunflower to sunflower to get closer. It was while Tiny was leaning over the edge of one particularly droopy sunflower, straining her ears to listen to the conversation, that she slipped. One moment her feet were firmly planted on the bright yellow petals. The next there was nothing but air between Tiny and the solid ground far below. She held her arms out, flapping them like a bird, feeling more scared than she'd ever been, but it was useless. Her arms couldn't help her as she fell down, down, down.

At the very last minute, a large butterfly swooped and caught Tiny, gliding her gently towards the ground. Tiny's fear turned to wonder. She felt the wind swoop past her arms and legs, as though she was flying.

They landed on a grassy patch, and the butterfly paused, wiggling its antennae.

"Thank you so much for saving me!" said Tiny breathlessly. Her heart was fluttering as she imagined what would have happened had she not been caught.

The butterfly glided away then, without a word.

Tiny could hear the animals speak clearly from here, because she had landed next to where they were gathered.

"Wow," Tiny said aloud. "I travelled all this way!" It was the furthest she had ever been before – even further than the blueberry bush – thanks to the butterfly.

Then she crouched down and listened
to the animals' conversation.

"She's unnatural…

Unwelcome…

Un—"

"We get

your point,"

said the frog

sternly. Tiny

could tell it was

him because he was croaking. The previous

speaker, who it turned out was a bird,

spoke again.

"We can't have humans living in the

school garden. They'll ruin our home!"

Who are they talking about? Tiny wondered.

A few murmurs of agreement rumbled around the group.

"They steal nuts!" said the squirrel, who had bushy grey fur. "I've seen them do it, I have. And they don't even have tails!"

The frog let out a croaky sigh, his green skin glinting in the sunlight.

"Yes, but we can't just assume she's bad without good reason."

"I saw it myself!" said a mouse, her voice high-pitched and squeaky. "Our children were playing merrily in the sunflowers, minding their own business when that...

that…*human* yelled at them!"

The same prickly feeling from earlier spread across Tiny's chest as she realized the animals were speaking about *her*. They thought she was a human and that she didn't belong here. But this was *her* home too. She might be a little different… but she deserved a safe place to sleep, didn't she?

Tiny listened to the mean things the animals had to say about her, and how they planned to chase her away. But they never seemed to be able to make a decision, because they were all very different themselves and so they argued quite a bit.

It was when one of the birds called her
a human for the third time, that Tiny could
no longer contain the anger rolling around
her chest. She jumped right into the
middle of the animals and bellowed: "I AM
NOT A HUMAN, AND I AM NOT
GOING TO LEAVE."

Finally, all of the voices fell silent...
Because every single animal was busy
staring, open-mouthed, at Tiny.

CHAPTER 5

Run!

Up close, the grown-up mice were bigger than Tiny expected, and their teeth looked like they could hurt if they decided to bite.

"Ah, look who's here," said one of the birds darkly. "I suppose we'd better do it now…"

"Do what?" asked the squirrel, whose bushy tail was standing up on end.

"Get rid of her, of course," said another bird. It hopped a little closer to Tiny, fluttering its feathers.

"What…? Well…how will you do that?" The squirrel seemed uncertain, which gave Tiny a little hope. If they would only *listen* to her they would know she wasn't a human and that she wouldn't hurt them.

The bird leered over her. "Well, you're no bigger than a worm really… I could gobble you up whole!"

The three baby mice who had been
mean to Tiny earlier laughed.

"She's harmless," said the frog. He was
the only one who seemed to give Tiny a
chance.

"Oh, no she isn't," said a grown-up
mouse – one of the ones who had glared at

Tiny when she was halfway up the sunflower. "I've seen it myself. She acts just like those humans in the playground!"

"True, true," said the first bird who had spoken. "Well, that's decided then."

"What's decided?" asked the squirrel, who seemed as confused as Tiny was.

Though whatever it was they had decided,
it didn't seem good.

"We'll chase her away!" said the mice.

"Or feed her to our young!" said the
birds.

Tiny spun round and round trying to
keep up with each creature who spoke.
The angry prickling feeling in her chest

had changed, and
it was like a
knot had tied
itself around
her heart. She
was afraid, and
something told her she had

to leave quickly.

"This is ridiculous!" said the frog. "What is wrong with everyone?"

And, once more, all the animals started arguing about the best way to get rid of Tiny. It was lucky, really, that they couldn't seem to decide, because it gave her a chance to escape.

Tiny saw a gap between the birds and mice, towards the trees and away from her sunflower home. It was her only option.

She took a deep breath in through her nose, and held it for five seconds before letting it out of her mouth. Then she ran for the second time that day.

It took Tiny ages to run through the tall grass. It slowed her down as she tried to escape. At one point she turned round, still moving, to see if she was being chased. The animals were too busy arguing to notice her.

But then the squirrel caught her eye, pointed its paw in Tiny's direction and yelled, "She's getting away!"

Suddenly the school garden was a burst of feathers and pattering feet as all the animals stampeded towards Tiny.

"Oh no, oh no, oh no!" she squealed, stumbling as she tried to move faster. She

climbed over a tree root

that was taller

than

she was.

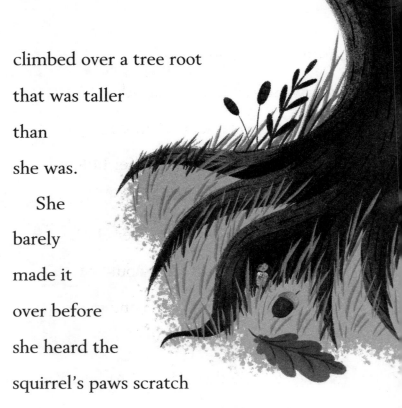

She

barely

made it

over before

she heard the

squirrel's paws scratch

against the wood as it scrambled after her.

Tiny was out of breath. She had only

run as far as three human strides, but it

had been like crossing a great big field

for her – one with lots of dangerous

hurdles in all directions.

Tiny tucked herself into the shadows beneath the tree root as the squirrel whisked past, not noticing her hiding place. Yet. She cursed herself for wearing such colourful sweet-wrapper clothes. If she were sensible, Tiny could have worn green or brown, to blend in with her surroundings. But she hadn't expected to have to hide from the other school garden animals.

Catching her breath, Tiny peered around, hoping to find something to help her blend in a bit better. She spotted an acorn nearby and darted to it. She dragged it back to the tree root, placing it over the crack she was hiding in. Curled up like this, Tiny was completely hidden from sight, and she peeked out from the side of the acorn to keep watch.

Perfect! Tiny thought, though moments later a rush of sadness washed over her. Her sunflower home was much more comfortable

and bright. Yet

here she was, curled up in the crack of a tree root, forced to hide because of who she was.

Not long after that, Tiny heard the pitter-patter of little feet, followed by a gasp, as the acorn was snatched from her. She looked up and let out a gasp of her own, because she was face to face with the squirrel, its fur standing on end like before. It didn't seem very happy to see her.

"Oh, it's you. You're not going to eat that, are you?" the squirrel asked, pointing to the acorn.

"Oh, no," Tiny answered. "I was just using it to hide."

The squirrel nodded, its fur falling into place again. Maybe it didn't mind her after all. Then, without warning, the squirrel lifted its head and yelled, "I've found the little human!"

But at the exact same moment, the school bell rang for break, and the animals gave up their search and scattered. This was the time of day the children would play in the school garden, and it wasn't safe for any of the creatures.

CHAPTER 6

Hide!

"Please don't tell them I'm here!" Tiny
begged, after the bell had stopped ringing.
The birds and mice had gone, so Tiny and
the squirrel were alone.

"Why shouldn't I?" said the squirrel,
but it didn't seem sure of the answer
itself. It wasn't nearly as threatening as
the birds.

Tiny thought about this for a moment. There wasn't really a good reason for the squirrel *not* to tell them.

"Well…" Tiny began.

"Well, what? Go on, I'm listening."

Then Tiny had an idea. "Well, the children will be here in a moment and they're sure to stomp on me with their shoes. You won't even *need* to tell everyone about me, because I'll be gone soon!" She said this a little too cheerily. Really, she didn't intend to get stomped on at all, but to carry on hiding so no creature spotted her.

The squirrel thought about this for

a moment, but it didn't seem convinced.

"And…" said Tiny, realizing something: the animals didn't even like each other, so they didn't *really* want to work together. "It'll take a very long time to round everyone up. Wouldn't you rather spend that time looking for more nuts, instead?"

That seemed to work, and the squirrel nodded. "I suppose I am late to guard my nuts. The children…they like digging and it can cause such a mess here. In my *home*."

Tiny nodded sympathetically.

"I bet it's awful."

"It is!" said the squirrel crossly, before adding, shyly. "Thank you for talking to me. You're really very lovely, no matter what the birds and mice say about you..."

Tiny almost asked the squirrel exactly what the birds and mice had been saying about her, but she had heard some of it, and didn't want to know more.

"Anyway," Tiny said, "I suppose you should go... And I'll wait here to

be stomped on…" Tiny really needed
the squirrel to leave so she could make
her escape.

The squirrel nodded,
before putting its
ears down.
"They won't
really
stomp on
you, will
they? I think
maybe if you
just keep hiding
and…well, don't make yourself known to
everyone…you could…stay…"

Tiny felt something warm in her chest now, but it wasn't anger this time.

"Alright, I'll do that," she grinned.

After the squirrel left, Tiny decided to hide as far away from it as possible, in case it changed its mind and told the birds after all. The children were slowly working their way into the woods to build dens and play hide-and-seek among the trees, so she needed to find somewhere safe.

"This has been such a long day already," Tiny said to herself with a sigh. She wondered if she would ever make it back home to her sunflower. "Maybe later, when all the animals are asleep…"

Tiny noticed the squirrel had left the top of the acorn behind. She decided to use it as a hat. Then if she crouched down she would be completely covered and safe from prying human eyes. She moved as quickly as she could past the darting feet, feeling her whole world rumble and shake as the children ran and screeched around her.

It took Tiny quite a bit of time, and a lot of clever hiding, to make it to the vegetable patch. There, she climbed onto the earth beds, which reminded her a little of the sunflower row. It was comforting and far less scary than the giant forest of trees.

Much more Tiny-sized. She zigzagged
between stalks of corn and carrot tops,
eventually stopping in front of some pea
pods, which looked a little like caterpillar
cocoons.

Tiny bit into the bottom one and tore
it open, munching on one of the peas
inside, because she was very hungry, before
climbing inside the pod. It was the perfect
size for her.

"The birds will never find me here!"
Tiny said to herself, satisfied with her
hiding spot.

She would wait until later and then
return to her sunflower, where she would
make sure not to draw attention to herself
again. Maybe, once enough time had
passed, the animals would come to accept
her.

But things don't always go as we plan.
Tiny could see the wildflower meadow
in front of her. To the right of it was a
little clearing where the frog's pond sat.
It wasn't a fancy home: just a washing-
up bowl filled with water and a water lily

peeking out over the top. There was a
ramp, too, just the right size for the frog to
climb in and out.

Children were running round the little
pond, kicking a giant white-and-black
ball back and forth to one another. Tiny
watched them, mesmerized, though part
of her was worried the ball would fly at her
and land SPLAT. The ball *did* fly and land
splat, but not anywhere near Tiny.
It landed right in the frog's pond!

Water splashed out of the pond, which tipped on its side.

The water lily and ramp fell to the ground next to it. The frog's home was ruined.

"Poor thing," said Tiny, imagining how she'd feel if her sunflower had been crumpled up into little pieces. She was lucky the children were so careful around it, very different to the way they acted in the forest and here in the clearing by the wildflowers and vegetable patch. Now Tiny could understand, a little, why the animals were so worried she might be a human. They were afraid.

Just then, Tiny heard a sob.

"My pond!" screeched the frog. "My beautiful pond. Oh no, what'll I do?"

Tiny had promised the squirrel she would stay in hiding, but she couldn't ignore the frog and let him cry on his own. So, leaving the safety of the pea pod, Tiny jumped down and ran over to him.

CHAPTER 7

A Disaster

"Are you alright?" Tiny asked, rushing over to the frog, whose body was curled up small.

The frog paused for a moment, surprised to see her, before croaking, "Am I alright? What sort of a question is that? Of course, I'm not alright! My home has just been destroyed."

He let out another croaky sob that tore at Tiny's heart. Tiny didn't mind that the frog had snapped at her because he seemed very upset.

"You could share my home if you like?" Tiny said, before lowering her voice. "I'm not supposed to let the birds know, but I'm hiding in the vegetable patch and I plan on heading back to my sunflower a little later. There's plenty of room, and you get to sit up high with the sun beating down—"

Tiny was going to say lots more lovely things about her home, but the frog interrupted her, a little more gently this time.

"It's so kind of you to offer. Really, it is. But you see, I'm a frog..."

Tiny nodded. "Oh, I knew that." She smiled politely, not sure why the frog, who was obviously a frog from his croaky voice, springy legs and green skin, was telling her this. But there was lots about frogs Tiny still had to learn.

"Yes, well," the frog continued. "Frogs can't sit up high near the sun. We aren't like flowers, dear, we'll shrivel up and die!"

Tiny gasped. "That sounds horrible!"

The frog nodded sadly. "It's why I'm so distressed. My pond is the only place in the entire school garden that's filled with water. If I'm away from a water source for too long, well, as I said, I'll—"

He didn't say the words, but Tiny understood. "Oh, we can't let that happen!"

The frog seemed cheered to have someone on his side. "Well, don't worry, you have enough to think about with the

birds and those pesky mice… The squirrel, she—"

"Actually, the squirrel was lovely," interrupted Tiny, thinking back to how she had let her escape. "She has promised to keep me a secret from the others."

The frog let out a croak that sounded sympathetic. "And I'll do the same. Now, I'd love to chat but, unfortunately, I've got to figure out what to do before the sun gets to me. I'll get a bit groggy soon and the longer I go without water the more chance there is that I'll…well…"

Tiny gasped for the second time. "You can't figure this out on your own. I'll help!

Together, I'm sure we can push your pond back into place, and after that we just need to find some water."

Tiny sprang into action, and the frog did as she instructed, hopping over to the opposite side of the pond so they could push it together.

"Three…two…one…" Tiny counted backwards, before pushing with all of her might.

But the pond did not budge.

"Oh no, this won't work!" said Tiny, letting out her frustration. "We need more help... Look, Frog, you hide in the shade here, and I'll get Squirrel. I won't be long."

Tiny said this with confidence, but it was rather hot and sunny. And the forest was quite far away for Tiny after she'd been on such a long journey already. How could she cross quickly, before something happened to Frog?

The bell rang just then, signalling for the children to return inside. Tiny spotted a couple of them at the vegetable patch, tending to the crops the way Nour had tended to her sunflower. They were using a watering can to make sure the vegetables had enough to drink.

And they had just cleared some weeds too. Now they were picking up a wheelbarrow and turning it towards the forest.

This was Tiny's chance! She climbed up the wheel of the wheelbarrow, while the children had paused for a moment. Then, she settled just above it, but still out of sight. She couldn't help but think, as the ground rumbled beneath her, that not all of the children disrupted the school garden. Some of them, like the ones tending to the vegetable patch and sunflowers, helped it grow.

CHAPTER 8

In the Forest

It was dangerous in the forest for Tiny, which was where she landed after hopping off the wheelbarrow. The birds were right above her, feeding their hungry young. And if they found her, she might be their next meal!

The mice were nearby, too, just on the grassy patch between the forest and her sunflower home.

Tiny looked around in search of Squirrel, but she was nowhere to be seen. She tried hard to swallow down the panic that threatened to bubble up in her chest. Would Frog cope on his own without Tiny to help him?

"Squirrel?" Tiny called, quietly at first, fear holding her back. But her voice grew steadily louder. "Squirrel!"

Suddenly, something tumbled into Tiny, and she thought it must be a bird, before Squirrel squeaked, *"Be quiet!"*

"Sorry," Tiny said sheepishly, turning to her.

"What are you doing?" Squirrel whispered angrily. "I told you to *hide* and instead you're out in the open *yelling* at me."

"I'm not yelling *at* you," Tiny pointed out. "I'm yelling *for* you."

"And why's that?" asked Squirrel. Quickly, Tiny explained that Frog was in trouble.

Squirrel moved fast, the way she always did, rushing towards Frog and his empty pond.

"Wait!" Tiny called, jogging behind Squirrel, but barely keeping up. She took several strides for each one of Squirrel's.

When Squirrel returned to her, Tiny was
out of breath, and a stitch was building in
her side. "I can't…run…as…fast…as…
you," she said between breaths.

"But I need you to help with the pond!"
Squirrel said.

"I know," Tiny
said desperately.
"Maybe you
could let
me…ride
on your
back?"

Squirrel looked at her horrified. "The birds were right. You *are* such trouble, Tiny."

Tiny's face fell. She knew the animals hadn't warmed to her, but she couldn't help being who she was.

"Oh, I'm sorry, Tiny. I didn't mean it, I swear," said Squirrel almost at once. "Here, climb on. I don't mind really."

She really did look sorry about what she'd said, so Tiny decided to forgive her. And together, they hurried back to Frog.

Galloping across the school gardens was unlike anything Tiny had experienced

before. The breeze zipped past her face,
cooling her down in the heat. All of the
sights blurred into a rainbow of colour, and
the sounds felt far away, as if Tiny was in a
world of her own.

When they arrived, things had taken
a turn for the worse. Frog could barely
move, which meant there was no way he
could help push the pond back into place.
And it quickly became clear that even
working together, Tiny and Squirrel were
too weak to do it on their own.

"We need the mice," Tiny said eventually, glancing at Frog. He wasn't saying much, and anything he did say was rather garbled: "Ribbet... Croaaaak... Ribbet... Croaaak..."

"But what if they tell the birds you're still here?" said Squirrel.

"I don't care!" Tiny said, realizing she was no longer afraid. Not when Frog might… She couldn't even think the words, much less say them. "We have to try."

Squirrel hopped from leg to leg. "Ohhh, I don't like this. I don't like any of it. But I'll get them. Maybe once they're here they won't mind so much. You stay with Frog."

Tiny nodded. It was good to have someone else to help her, especially as Frog seemed more muddled and confused by everything around him the longer he was

out of water. And it really was very hot…

While Tiny waited, she decided to search around to see if she could find any water. It might give them more time to sort out the pond. That was when she remembered the watering can by the vegetable patch, next to the wheelbarrow she had climbed earlier.

"Wait here!" said Tiny to Frog as she jogged towards it.

Frog just replied with, "*Ribbet…croak… ribbet…*" which Tiny took to mean, "Alright, see you soon."

The watering can towered over Tiny like a great big building over a human. There was no way she would be able to get all the way up to the top of it. But a few little droplets were falling out of the holes at the spout, each as large as a pea. Tiny found a fallen leaf nearby, and spread it beneath the droplets, letting it gather with water before dragging the leaf to Frog.

"Here, this might help a little," said Tiny, encouraging Frog to roll over the leaf.

But all Frog could say was, "*Croaaaaak*."

"Hurry up, Squirrel," Tiny said desperately, as she rushed back to the watering can for more.

It was on her third trip that Tiny heard the pitter-patter of lots of little feet coming closer, and relief washed over her as she realized Squirrel had managed to convince the mice to help.

"You can do this," Tiny said to herself, standing in front of the sideways pond and practising what she had planned to say to the mice when they arrived.

CHAPTER 9

Helping Frog

The mice rushed to Frog, not noticing
Tiny at first, and so she cleared her throat
awkwardly to let them know she was there.

The first grown-up mouse turned round
and opened her mouth wide. But before she
could let out a scream, Tiny spoke.

"WAIT!" she said, just as a rumble of
thunder sounded up above.

The mice looked between Tiny and the sky.

"She made that happen!" said one of the little mice.

"Wow!" said another. "Do it again!"

Tiny opened her mouth to speak once more but instead of words, another rush of thunder sounded.

All the mice fell silent, watching her.

"I know you all think I'm a human," Tiny said, "and that I'll destroy the school garden the way some of the children do."

"*Some* of the children," said the mouse who had nearly screamed. "What do you mean *some* of the children? They're all

bad! Every one of them."

"They're not," said Tiny, thinking of
Nour reading her book in the mornings,
and tending to her sunflower so carefully.
Then she thought of the children who
had helped the vegetables grow. She told
the mice everything she'd seen. "There's
no way, of course, to prove I'm a good
neighbour, except...well, time."

"Thyme?" asked one of the mice. "We
have some of that in the wildflower garden,
where the herbs grow."

"No, I mean *time*," said Tiny. "If you
just let me stay for a little longer, I'll show
you I'm not bad."

The mice peered at one another.

It seemed no one knew what to say.

That was when Squirrel spoke.

"Tiny was the one who came to get me to help Frog," she said. "She risked her life to save Frog, even though you were planning on feeding her to the baby birds."

The mice lowered their ears a little guiltily, as a third rumble of thunder sounded.

"I suppose we could wait," said one of the mice. "But if you so much as squish a single blueberry you'll have to leave!"

Tiny nodded. "I'm sure I can agree to that," she said, feeling a little relieved. It was a start. "Now, let's help Frog!"

With her words, another rumble sounded from the sky, as if letting them all know they needed to set to work. Frog was lying very still, his eyes half open. Tiny could see his stomach moving with slow, steady breaths, and she knew they needed to hurry.

Tiny, Squirrel, the three little mice and their mothers lifted with all of their might, and together they managed to push Frog's

pond back into place and put the ramp

where it belonged.

"Yippee!" said the mice.

"Yippee!" said Squirrel.

"Yippee!" said Tiny, thinking how lovely it was to all work as a team.

"How will we fill the pond?" asked Squirrel, reminding Tiny that they couldn't celebrate yet. She peered up to the sky where lightning flashed, followed by another sound of thunder.

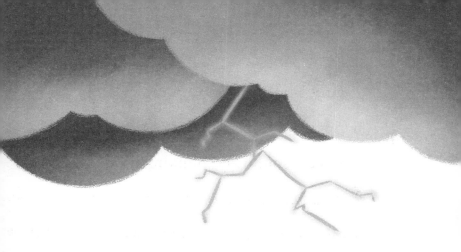

The clouds were a dark grey colour, gathering together tightly.

"I think, if we're lucky, it's going to rain!" said Tiny, noticing the air had cooled down a little.

Rain was a wonderful thing in the school garden: it meant the flowers were nourished, the soil kept damp, and right now it meant Frog's pond could fill up again.

As Tiny, Squirrel and the mice watched the sky, hoping for rain (the mice even did a little dance round the pond to encourage it), several dots appeared in the distance, getting bigger and bigger and bigger.

Tiny realized, a little too late, that the birds were coming.

CHAPTER 10

Home Time

"What is going on?" said one of the birds, the most confident one from earlier. The others stood just slightly behind it, following its lead.

It was Squirrel who stepped forward, blocking Tiny with her body. "We're helping Frog with his pond," she said.

The birds peered past Squirrel's

shoulder at Tiny, and she stared back. She refused to be chased away from her home, even if they were going to feed her to their young.

"And what is that human doing here?" asked the bird. Its voice was very calm, but there was something menacing about it. Fluttering its feathers in annoyance, it stared at Tiny with a beady eye.

"Her name is Tiny," said one of the baby mice. "And she is *not* a human."

"Hush," said one of the mother mice, pulling her child behind her.

She seemed afraid of the birds, Tiny realized. In fact, all of the animals did.

It's not fair, thought Tiny. *The birds seem to be in charge of the school garden, but all they've done is keep the animals apart. We should all live and work together.*

"You don't have to listen to them, you know," said Tiny, turning to the mice and Squirrel. Frog was lying very still now, and Tiny was scared of what was going to happen to him. But, as she spoke, she felt the first splash of rain land and splatter in front of her. The droplet was much bigger for Tiny than it would be for a human.

The animals all peered up at the sky.

"RAIN!" squealed Tiny, forgetting about the birds and everyone else, because rain meant that Frog was going to be saved. The droplets splashed all around Tiny, soaking her. It was a relief after such a hot day.

"Hold on one moment," said a bird, flapping its wings. But Squirrel and the mice formed a little half circle to protect Tiny as she rushed to Frog.

Frog was curled up like an autumn leaf, but Tiny watched as the water refreshed his skin. She caught some droplets in her hands and poured them over Frog. It took her much longer than it took the bumblebees to collect pollen. But, slowly, the rain picked up pace, helping Tiny with her mission.

The droplets were growing larger and the wind more fierce. Tiny was finding it difficult to be out in this weather without

the droplets knocking her to the floor, and
the wind whisking her away.

"You have to take cover!" Squirrel said,
coming up beside Tiny and shielding her
with her tail. "The rain is too big for you.
It'll hurt you!"

"I have to make sure Frog is alright," said Tiny stubbornly, as she tended to her friend.

As they watched, Frog's back legs twitched first. Then his front. And he hopped up and down to show he was feeling better.

"Oh, how lovely this rain is!" he said, and Tiny's heart swelled to see him back to his normal self again.

"Frog, you're okay!" said Tiny. "And look, your pond is back upright. It'll fill up in no time with all the rain!"

"Thank you, Tiny," said Frog, once he'd caught up with everything that had happened. "Now you must get to some shelter. Pop by later when the rain has stopped, will you?"

Tiny nodded. "I will, I promise."

Tiny climbed on Squirrel's back,
then they sprinted through the wildflower
garden and into the forest.

"What happened to the birds?" Tiny asked. She had completely forgotten to be afraid of them while she'd been busy looking after her friend.

"They realized that with you in our ranks, they're outnumbered," said Squirrel cheerily. "They're going to have to stop bossing us all around now. You've made things better round here already!"

"You have, Tiny," agreed the mice. "We're so sorry we were awful to you before."

Tiny smiled. She knew they were just afraid of things changing, but they'd come together when it mattered.

After the rain had stopped, Tiny returned with Squirrel to check on Frog. She saw the birds had returned Frog's water lily back to his pond.

"Everyone worked together," said Frog proudly. "To save *me* of all creatures. But really, Tiny, it started with you."

Tiny returned to her sunflower with a special pebble which Frog found near his pond. The pebble looked blue-green in the sunlight, and Tiny placed it at the bottom of her sunflower, to mark her home.

"Come on, then!" Tiny said to the baby mice. "Would you like to visit my home?"

The mice surrounded Tiny's sunflower, as they all climbed together, one leaf at a time, to the top. In the distance, they saw the schoolchildren leave for the day. Tiny even spotted Nour with her book still tucked in her arms.

Tiny and the mice waved goodbye to the children and looked forward to their next adventure in the school garden, where they would play together as friends.

With thanks to...

**The Society of Authors for supporting
Aisha Bushby in the writing of this book with
their Authors' Foundation Grant.**

Sarah Cronin
Safae El-Ouahabi
Jessica Feichtlbauer
Anne Finnis
Beth Gooding
Helen Greathead
Alice Moloney
Will Steele
Kübra Teber
Claire Wilson

And everyone else who has
supported this book.